T0148642

Dream Drifter

Daniel Thompson, Sr.

Order this book online at www.trafford.com
or email orders@trafford.com

Most Trafford titles are also available at major online book retailers.

Printed in the United States of America.

isbn: 978-1-4907-4636-4 (sc)
isbn: 978-1-4907-4638-8 (hc)
isbn: 978-1-4907-4637-1 (e)

Library of Congress Control Number: 2014916244

Trafford rev. 09/10/2014

www.trafford.com
North America & international
toll-free: 1 888 232 4444 (USA & Canada)
fax: 812 355 4082

Acknowledgment

I would like to thank Jesus Christ; my wife, Fay Thompson; my mother, Eugenia Thompson; my sons, Daniel and Demetrius Thompson; and Capt. Jill Clark for their support over the years.

People make many journeys in their lifetime, but they make even more in their mind. These journeys can prove to be bizarre or inexplicable and have no way of manifesting themselves to fruition—or can they? There is a very thin line between dreams and reality—a whole other world that we cannot see. Ergo, in the inner mind lie unspeakable horrors. There lies a realm that is indistinguishable. Whether fact or fiction, you must come to terms with its existence or nonexistence. Apropos, only you can control the power of its destruction! Only you can control its inevitability!

Chapter 1

One day, in the summer of 1964—about three o'clock in the morning—as a young boy, I had awakened to go to the bathroom. Obviously, I was not fully awake, because when returning to my bedroom, I paused in the hallway and noticed my reflection on my sister's closet door. The closet door was very shiny, and it was very easy to see the reflections. As I gazed at my reflection, an image formed on the door and appeared to look exactly like me at first, but then I noticed that the image started to change. The figure was about the same size as I was. Alarmingly, a horrible transformation occurred. The figure on the door took the form a glowing red demon that hideously glared back at me. It was very lifelike when it moved and seemed as if it were going to lunge at me. In horror, I ran into my bedroom as fast as I could and leaped into my bed facedown, clinging to my bed as tight as I could. I didn't move. I didn't flinch.

However, my heart was racing extremely fast. I feared that this thing was real as I laid there in my bed with my eyes tightly shut. I finally had fallen asleep. When I had awakened the next morning, I found myself trembling about the occurrence. The light of morning eventually gave me solace. However, I continued to ponder about the image. I still didn't know if it were real or if I were losing my mind.

My name is Danny. I was just six years old during an encounter with my first apparition. I lived in a little town in the northeast, with my mother, father, and three siblings. For years, I wondered about it. Even now, I still don't know if it were real or imaginary. But it doesn't bother me anymore. It hadn't bothered me since my boyhood. But the apparitions did not end there.

Two years later, in 1966, in the same house, there was another occurrence. This time was far worse than the first. I was sleeping in the same bed as my younger brother Darryl because I lost my bed to my baby brother Paul who was too large for his crib that was in my parents' room in the front of the house on the second floor. So my parents had moved the three-year-old in with me and Darryl in the rear of the house on the second floor.

It was in the late summer, on one particular night, way past midnight, when Darryl was extremely restless. He tossed and turned in bed as if he were out of his mind. I was also restless on this hot summer night because of Darryl's constant rocking in bed.

"Darryl, stop! Stop rocking!" I exclaimed.

Darryl was rocking in bed so aggressively that he knocked me from out of bed, and I found myself on the floor. The floor was cool albeit I knew I couldn't stay there all night. And as I began to push myself upward to get back into bed, I saw a huge pair of the most grotesque, hairy feet that one could imagine right in front of me. I was frozen as I stared at the monstrous feet, trembling in fear of what I might find attached to them. I slowly followed the feet upward. The legs were just as hairy as the feet. Still trembling, I noticed that the image was extremely large and was wearing a very colorful and decorative garb, like a tribal African or Native American chief.

When I finally got up to the image's face, my heart stopped, for I saw the most hideous creature out of hell imaginable. The monster had an evil, grimacing grin, and its face was also hairy, similar to that of a gorilla. The thing glared down at me, looking at me dead in my eyes, but the creature did not move. I quickly hoisted myself back up into my bed, pressing and clinging with all of my might and not making any motion while seemingly holding my breath. I feared that the creature would devour me or, at best, rip me to pieces. My eyes were closed extremely tight, and my heart was racing really fast. I was frozen in this position until I fell asleep. Awakening the next morning, I didn't remember what happened until I was fully awake and cognizant.

As my thoughts cleared, I pondered to myself if the monster were real or imaginary, just as I had done two years prior. I came to the conclusion that it was real and would be back that night to destroy me. I dared not speak about it to my parents or siblings until years later.

Chapter 2

Some years had passed. I finally told my brothers about the two occurrences, especially emphasizing the horror of the second encounter—the gorilla-like apparition. I never experienced anything like that again that was so lifelike. As I grew older, those two experiences faded as far as being a threat to me. I had hundreds of horrible dreams, but not many of them seemed like reality.

And as the 1960s came to an end, I had various types of dreams. Some had patterns and symbolic meanings; some were incredibly horrific but only happened once, and some were recurring sequels. For instance, I frequently dreamed I mysteriously appeared in the middle of strange, wide-open fields that went on for miles and miles in both directions, with endless trees in the front and back of the fields. Both directions looked exactly the same. The fields were identical to that of the fields in the motion picture *The Wizard of Oz,* where Dorothy, the Scarecrow, the Tin Man, and Cowardly Lion escape out of the woods and into these glorious fields in which the Wicked Witch of the West had sent poppies to put them to sleep, but the good witch Glenda sent snow to awake them to proceed to the Emerald City, which was closely in their view.

When I had trekked in either direction of these fields, which ultimately had their end, I saw a lighthouse off at a distance in each direction as I was approaching the end. But as I approached the ends of each direction, the lighthouses vanished. The funny thing is that there weren't any oceans or any kinds of bodies of water anywhere to be a reason for the lighthouses. And there weren't any people, animals, birds, or insects anywhere as I walked in each direction. There wasn't even a slight wind blowing. Each time that I mysteriously appeared on these fields, I was faced with the dilemma of which direction I should take. Both ways seemed pleasant enough at first, and it was always sunny when I started out. Once I made up my mind on the direction I chose, I had hoped I made the right decision.

As I journeyed on for a while, the sun would start to set, and the fields disappeared. And I walked through a porthole of some sort. It had immediately turned to night on the other side of the porthole even though the sun was just beginning to set on the other side. This was the frequent happening until I proceeded farther into town.

The very first time, the townspeople at the entrance of the city seemed friendly enough; however, none of them even noticed me until I arrived deep into the bowels of the city. This was the very first time after leaving the fields. When I arrived in the heart of the town, strange things happened. Now, for sure, I knew I had taken the wrong direction.

This area of the town resembled my hometown. As I walked into an area of town that looked exactly like Parkside, where I grew up, I encountered an evil witch. She followed me from the air as she flew around, waving in and around the trees, making a funky, shrilly sound as if I had disturbed her. She terrorized me as I tried to find my way back to the porthole. I ventured around the town desperately trying to avoid her, for she was awfully annoying, following me almost everywhere I went. And when I had managed to evade her, somehow she found me to terrorize the hell out of me again.

For some strange reason, the witch would not follow me down the actual street that resembled Kenwood Avenue, where my house was in Parkside—for which it was named, because it was a forest. Most of the town was enveloped in darkness during the daylight hours due to the overabundance of trees. There were only a few streets in Parkside where the sun actually shined. My street just happened to be one of them. I soon discovered that the witch would not follow me there, not even at night.

My aunt and cousins (the Wades) also lived in Parkside, the next street over but two blocks back. When I attempted to visit them on Langham Avenue from dusk to night, she would wait for me at the end of my street, where Kenwood met Park Boulevard, which was one of the longest and darkest streets in Parkside. When she had waited for some time, hiding in the trees, and noticed that I didn't come down that way, she would fly way above the houses and try to spot me that way. Once she spotted me, she swooped down and tried to bite and claw me. But somehow I managed to keep from getting hurt, especially by getting to Haddon Avenue, which was one of the busiest streets in Camden. This particular street was one of the few streets in the entire city that had very few trees. The witch hated Haddon Avenue because during the day, it was too bright for her, and at night, there were too many passersby walking about that could possibly assist me, and she did not want to have any altercations with anyone other than me.

"I don't know what I did to make her angry, but she only comes after me," I said to myself.

After being chased down many dark streets in Parkside, I was able to get back to the real world and escape this realm of the dream world without even finding the porthole that I came through to get to that strange town. Now, seeming to be forever trapped here, I concentrated with tremendous brainpower to get myself back to the real world, and I never encountered the witch again.

Chapter 3

I had a strong bond with my little brother Paul. Of all my siblings, Paul's dream experiences were the most similar to mine although his dreams never took him much farther than our neighborhood. My dreams, however, took me to various places in the world and other dimensions.

One night, Paul dreamed that light reflections on our bedroom wall were haunting him. The bright lights were flickering constantly and making horrible sounds. Paul's mind was being tortured, so I told him that I would protect him because I saw the images as well. Paul felt relieved since I took ownership of the problem.

"Don't be afraid, Paul, I won't let them do anything to you," I said.

Like mine, Paul's dreams took him to the cellar beneath the basement of our home in Camden, only to find another level where a hideous creature enjoyed frightening the hell out of us.

In 1970, I was twelve years old and had a series of nightmares. The things underneath the basement were not interested in anyone else in my family but my brother Paul and I.

Somehow I managed to find myself trapped in the basement by a particular monster, which would bar my way and keep me from getting upstairs to safety. While ducking and diving from this monster, I thought of another way to outmaneuver the creature. There was a trapdoor in our basement that I had to escape to because there were more hiding places there. It seemed crazy for me to go deeper into the bowels of the house, but it helped me lure the monster to that level and gave me a greater chance for escape. I was able to trick the monster to come to the lower level under the basement by allowing him to chase me into the catacombs of the cellar; however, I didn't know how long it would be before the creature would find its way back to the first level or even the kitchen, which terrified me.

More months passed, and I was about to turn age thirteen. I was starting to grow into a young man and was feeling my oats, becoming proud (watching Bruce Lee, Jim Brown, and Fred Williamson movies), which made me become more macho and less afraid of monsters and ghouls.

Chapter 4

During this time, the Vietnam War was still in effect. This was a war I thought was never going to end—starting in 1955 and ending in 1975. It was getting close to my time to go, but I missed going to war by one year. My friend Gregory, who was two years older than I, became very concerned. We would sit on the roof of his garage and talk about the war and how close it was getting to our time. We were horrified with the fact that if the war didn't end soon, we would be next in line. We also talked about the horrors of nuclear war between United States and Russia. I was extremely afraid of this possibility.

This was a time when I had other encounters from another menacing monster in the basement of my house, which was similar to the previous basement monster but a lot shorter. This monster haunted me for many years whereas the previous creature attacked me only once, and I never encountered it again. Whenever I was watching TV at night, downstairs in the living room, and the kitchen light was turned off—a frizzy, black-haired, short creature would peer out; part of its head I could see from the corner of my eye. And as soon as I looked in the direction of the monster, it would duck its head back in. So I barely got a glimpse of the thing. I was scared, but I thought, as long as my family were downstairs with me, the hideous beast would never try to approach me.

The living room was the first room in the house when entering the front door. There was no foyer. To the right was the staircase that led upstairs to three bedrooms, and looking straight ahead from the front door, the living room led into the dining room. But the kitchen was perpendicular to the dining room and, to the right, separated by a threshold. Directly in back of the kitchen was the door that led to the basement. For years, there was no lock on the door, which terrified me. Even when my sisters and brothers were watching TV with me, the monster would be looking for me by showing its awful silhouette right at the threshold. During those days, I didn't mention the monster to anyone in my family except for my little brother Paul until many years later, for fear of being committed. And no one ever encountered the monster except me, until Jesus Christ and my mother Gina intervened after I yelled out for them on two separate occasions where they saved me from getting devoured.

As I was running away from the monster, from the basement door, I ran as fast as I could to get upstairs, but I seemingly was running in slow motion, and when I got to the stairs that led to the upstairs bedrooms, the monster had gained on me and got in front of me, barring my way from getting upstairs, and Jesus appeared in between me and the monster. The monster trembled in fear of God destroying it before its time and instantly vanished. And on another occasion, my mother ran downstairs, pulled me from the creature's clutches from another chase and screamed at the monster to leave me alone, causing it to creep back into the basement. Many evenings, I looked over toward the kitchen, and I saw the shadow of the evil monster, but the thing never made a move as long as my family was there with me.

Chapter 5

When I turned age fourteen in 1972, I became a freshman in high school and was considered to be the man of the house by everyone in my family, especially since my mother and father had separated three years prior. Now, I was solely responsible for making sure all of the windows and doors were locked properly and that all lights were turned off at night to conserve energy. The basement door now had a latch on it, but sometimes the screws became loose, threatening the integrity of its security.

This was now a new responsibility for me, and I started to feel a little afraid again. I had an eerie feeling about locking up and turning off all the lights downstairs on the first floor before going upstairs to bed. My nightly routine was to make rounds downstairs. I made sure the front doors and windows were locked. I locked the screen door and then the main door, securing all of the locks that were on the doors. I made sure all the windows were locked. Then I proceeded to the kitchen through the dining room and locked the back screen door, the main door, and the back windows in the same manner as I had done in the front of the house. And, finally, I made sure the door leading down to the basement was locked. A lot of time, this is where I incurred the problem, either because the latch on the door was loose or busted from its constant usage from everyone doing their own laundry in the basement, or because someone almost always left the lights on in the basement, particularly the light in the rear of the basement. So I couldn't very well lock the basement door with the lights still on. That would have been very irresponsible of me.

The light at the beginning of the basement was not a problem, as long as it was working, since I could turn that light off from the kitchen. It was the light in the rear of the basement that caused me to have anxiety because it had to be turned off manually by pulling a little cord affixed to it, and the light was mounted from the ceiling. Now, most of the time, this light was left on by accident by one of my family members who were just being forgetful. And I had discussed this with all of them. But it still continued. No matter, because at the end of the night, it was still my responsibility to turn it off to help my mother (Gina) save energy and keep the electric bill as low as possible.

The real problem was that the light at the front of the basement was either out or missing a lot of the time because someone decided to use it for their room, or it was on the verge of going out anyway. And we had a problem purchasing additional bulbs for the basement since we were on a very tight budget. This posed as a very big problem because I would have to turn off the light at the back of the basement, leaving the basement very dark, with only the dim kitchen light to give any illumination. I couldn't see very well. Now, sometimes, not only was the basement light not working in the front of the basement, but the kitchen light would blow out as well, making the only working light the one in the rear of the basement. Now it was pitch-black when I turned off the only working light until I got to the dining room. But I would never let my mother down. I could have left the light on and ran upstairs like a coward, but I didn't. I couldn't. I was compelled to stay, compelled to utterly obey and make good with my mother, who was supporting six children by herself.

With no assistance from my father or anyone except God, my mother had to work two and, sometimes, three jobs to support me, my sisters (Lana and Yvonne), and my brothers (Darryl, Paul, and Robert). Yvonne and Robert were the babies and were always right under her wing. I did everything possible to help my mother and my siblings. So regardless of how afraid I would become, I somehow managed to suck it up, do my family's bidding, and try to support them the best way I could. I had a job on a paper route two years prior, but it didn't last very long because the customers seldom paid me even though I diligently delivered their newspapers. I turned in what money I had and took a loss every week.

On several occasions, I found myself in frightening positions. On one particular night, I was watching TV with my sisters and brothers downstairs in the living room, which had a very dim light from the two lamps that were there. I was distracted by the shadow that appeared at the threshold that led into the kitchen. And as I said before, I never saw this shadow if the kitchen light was on. It was just a dark shadow that seemed to intermittently appear but seemed to linger for a spell while making extremely slow movements. I could see this when I looked back at the kitchen, but when I looked back at the TV, a dark, furry image would peer out. When I looked back in the direction of the TV, the image would quickly move back into the darkness of the kitchen. However, I managed to catch a glimpse of the thing before it was fully consumed by the seemingly pitch-blackness. These occurrences repeated almost every other night and for several years. The shadow specter kept me uneasy. And I dared not tell anyone about it. I didn't want to strike fear into my sisters and brothers.

One particular night in 1971, after having supper and doing my homework in the kitchen, I watched TV with my family as I often did. We had a big black-and-white wood stereo console TV with rabbit ears. It had a hi-fi for forty-five records and seventy-eight albums on one side and an AM/FM radio section on the other in the living room. My mother had worked extremely hard to purchase that TV for us. We had that TV for a really long time. Even after it stopped working, it was a piece of nice furniture, and we could still use the record player and the radio. It was repaired a couple of times, but it finally gave up the ghost.

About 8:30 p.m. or so, my mother would call for the younger children (Robert and Yvonne) to come upstairs to go to bed. Only me, Lana, Darryl, and Paul were allowed to stay up past eighty thirty, (ten o'clock on the weekdays and one o'clock on the weekends), and Lana rarely watched TV with us. She didn't like the television shows we watched, which were Westerns and action shows/movies. Darryl turned in early almost all of the time (about 9:00 p.m. or so, even on the weekend). So that left me and my brother Paul downstairs by ourselves. To my demise, I often fell asleep on the floor in the middle of a movie or TV show. Paul tried to awaken me several times but would finally give up.

"Danny, wake up!" said Paul.

"I'm awake! I'm awake!" I replied.

"If you're awake, what just happened in the movie?" said Paul.

I could never give Paul the correct answers and, after awhile, Paul became frustrated with me, because I kept falling asleep when I was supposed to be watching the movie or program with him. After going through this several times, Paul would leave me and go upstairs to bed, unbeknownst to me. And I always found myself all alone when I had awakened with the TV turned off and sometimes the living room lamps turned off as well. I looked around for Paul and saw nothing. I immediately looked at our big antique-looking clock mounted on the wall opposite the TV which I could barely make out because sometimes all I had was the brightness of the moonlight coming through the living room window. It was usually very late, somewhere around twelve o'clock midnight or much later. When I finally realized that I was truly by myself, I was compelled to look toward the threshold of the kitchen, expecting to see the dark, eerie shadow of the monster or the monster itself. Sometimes, I saw nothing as I stared in that direction, and sometimes I would see the frightening shadow, but I wouldn't move. And the most dreadful of all—sometimes I saw the creature glaring back at me before it made its move to come after me (whether the living room lamps were on or not). Sometimes it was more aggressive than other times. Then, when it came after me, I ran upstairs where the monster never came unless it was just to the steps where it could see through the railing at my mother's bedroom if she had her door opened. But it never came all the way upstairs because it was afraid of my mother. However, regardless of being chased, I would make sure those lamps were turned off and every door and window locked before I came upstairs even if it meant waiting out the monster until it went back into the basement. But I sometimes had a sense for when it went back down to the basement. And the latch on the basement door provided no guarantee that the door would remain locked. But it was all we had. I had tightened the screws every time I got a chance.

Even though I was concerned about conserving energy to keep my mother's light bill low, I briefly turned on both living room lamps and the dining room chandelier as I hesitated toward the kitchen at the back of the house. Sometimes if the light was on in the kitchen, it was so dim. I couldn't tell if it was even on until I got in there. And sometimes the kitchen light blew out as well. As soon as I approached the threshold, I always expected something to jump out at me. Sometimes, it did. But on this particular night, nothing happened. I proceeded to lock the kitchen doors (the screen door, the interior door, and the basement door). We all called it the cellar door.

"Just as I thought," I said to myself.

The basement light was on in the back of the basement, where I had to pull the little chain on the ceiling fixture to turn it off. Now the only illumination I had was that of the dim kitchen light. I made my way back to the front of the basement, but I felt very scared when heading back to the stairs that led me up to the kitchen. I felt like something was right at my back, but I dared not turn around. I managed to make it all the way to the top of the stairs and proceeded to close and lock the kitchen door, but it would not close. A force from the other side of the door prevented me from closing the door. The harder I pushed, the harder it pushed. The thing pushed so hard that I fell backward. As I was struggling to get back on my feet, I heard a low-based growl. An ugly beast darted out from behind the kitchen door, and I ran as fast as I could. I tried to make it upstairs where my family was, but for some strange reason, I was running in slow motion, as if some force were pulling me backward. The creature was right on my tail. And I struggled trying to run, but I made it upstairs to my mother's room where the beast dared not follow. Monsters were afraid of my mother and occasionally felt their oats to attempt to come up the stairs but not all the way up. I was safe for another night, but I knew there would be other nights I would be confronted by evil creatures.

Chapter 6

In the year 1973, I turned fifteen, and my dreams went off on a tangent. I journeyed from Philadelphia to New York on several occasions. The cities were very similar by comparison to me, so similar that sometimes I was confused about which city I was in. I told my little brother, Paul, that I was going to take a trip, but I didn't tell him where.

"I'm going to see the world!" I said to my brother Paul.

"Me too!" Paul replied.

But Paul was only ten years old, and I thought he was too young to travel.

"Which places would you like to see, Paul?" I asked.

"I don't know, but I know there has to be a lot of exciting places out there, more exciting than Camden," Paul replied.

So I made my first journey out of the small city of Camden into the huge city of Philadelphia. In order to do this, I had to cross the grim and creepy Benjamin Franklin Bridge by foot.

At first, my journey was mundane and simple. And as I approached the middle of the bridge, I could no longer proceed straightaway on the street level because some strange force barred my way—a wall that I could not penetrate. So I proceeded to walk up the narrow, steel railing that must have ascended at least seven hundred feet upward into the dark night sky. The bridge peeked to an arc hovering over the dark and tumultuous Delaware River and descended downward into the more urban sections of Philadelphia and Camden. This journey was in no way uneventful, for the steal railing of the icy cold bridge swayed and wiggled like rope as I walked on it. I was indeed frightened; however, I maintained my composure and managed to get to the Pennsylvania side alive. There was no force to impede me at that height.

Now I walked around in the city of Philadelphia for a while. It was very late at night, and hardly no one was walking the streets. As I ventured on, I found myself approaching the banks of the Hudson River of New York, not the Delaware River as it should have been. I started to freak out a little bit. I questioned how I could have ended up near the Hudson River and not the Delaware River when they distanced about a hundred miles apart. Peering off at a distance, I could see the Statue of Liberty in all of her splendor. I continued walking, and the streets became the streets of New York, not Philly.

"How did I get all the way up here?" I said to myself.

"I must find my way back to Camden!" I said.

The World Trade Center was still under construction, and I never saw the Empire State Building during my journey as tall as that building is. As I kept walking, I ended up back in Camden in a matter of minutes without crossing the Benjamin Franklin Bridge a second time. I knew this was totally impossible, because of the one hundred–mile distance of these two cities. Perplexed as I was, I managed to shake off the mental anguish I was feeling because of the illogical thing that just happened on this journey, surely knowing that even more bizarre experiences lay ahead.

Now, while walking down the streets of Camden, I miraculously appeared in the "fields" again, as if I were somehow zapped there. Looking in both directions, all I could see were miles and miles of gorgeous, plush fields of very green grass and daisies with beautifully manicured tall hedges, which seemed likes walls on each side of the fields at a great distance apart. More often than not, my travels from the "fields" took me to incredibly strange places.

For instance, I traveled into a strange town through a mysterious porthole at the end of the "fields." The town was a torn-down old slum. Every building was awfully dirty, and there weren't any people there. As I walked farther on, I saw an old abandoned school, and the color of it was of an austere gray and brown. The playground of the school showed broken remnants of swings and sliding boards. I went into the school and walked around. I saw an old gymnasium where the showers still remained, but they were filthy and very old. When I left the gym, I bumped into a very pretty girl, who was a teenager just like me. I asked her what her name was.

"My name is Donna, what is your name?" she replied in a real polite manner.

"My name is Danny, where is everybody, and what are you doing here all by yourself?" I asked.

Donna just stared at me and didn't respond. She slowly approached me and gazed into my eyes, which was extremely mesmerizing. She took my arms and put them around her waist and kissed me on the mouth. I never flinched and kissed her right back—a complete stranger. Then Donna said, "Would you like to do me?"

I paused as if I were frozen. I was starting to lose my cool and stammered. "What? Yes, I would!" I said.

Donna then backed away from me and started running.

"Donna, where are you going?" I exclaimed.

"You're gonna have to catch me to find out!" she shouted.

So I ran after her. She was real fast. I lost her for a while. The longer it took me to find her, the more apprehensive I became. And it was difficult for me to run in that condition. After about twenty minutes of searching, Donna surfaced. She sneaked up from behind me and threw her arms around me. We kissed and hugged, but I hugged her too hard because she soon crumbled in my arms and turned into a pile of powder. I was sad and walked through the streets of the barren slum with my head hanging down, and a force snatched me up and transported me back to Camden.

Chapter 7

One night, in the year 1974, my little brother Paul and I were getting ready for bed. As we were conversing in our bunk beds, we noticed we had another thing in common when it came to dreams. Before falling asleep, we stared at the wall in our respective beds, and it soon became a panoramic view —a movie screen if you will (in full color). My first vision on the wall was that of an old country fair taking place, with rides and all kinds of folk dressed up in colorful garb, as if they were from the 1800s.

Everyone was having a tremendously good time. And then, everything went a blur. Then there was a transition when the panoramic visions on the wall turned into real dreams, but I could not differentiate the two. I had other dreams on the wall. Although they never made any sense to me, not one of them was horrific or morbid. I cherished the times I was able to have the vivid dreams on the wall. However, I soon forgot all about them. After several months, I could no longer dream on the wall, no matter how hard I tried. I soon gave up trying.

The deeper I got into puberty, the more sexual in nature my dreams became. Even though I was a raised a devout Catholic and almost became an altar boy, I never really tried to resist having the sexual dreams because I liked having them. However, I did try to fight the demonic ones as did my younger brother Darryl. My brother was having nightmares so bad that he removed the golden cross that my mother had hanging from our living room wall near the front door. Apparently, Darryl thought that by having the cross with him at night and putting it at the foot of his bed would ward off any demonic presence and keep him from having horrible dreams, or as our little brother Paul called them, "nighttime mare." But it didn't. In fact, Darryl's dreams got even worse, so he later put the cross back on the wall.

One day, Darryl went outside to play on what started out as a nice, sunny day, only to learn that a strange creature was terrorizing our neighborhood. It was a bright red horse with red glowing eyes as if fire was shooting out of them. The evil horse galloped around our neighborhood and found its way to the alley behind our house. Darryl made eye contact with the demonic horse as it galloped back and forth through the alley. The hellish beast charged at Darryl, but fortunately, Darryl managed to get inside our house through the backdoor from the alleyway before the horse could get him. My brother thought that was the end of it, but he was dead wrong. As Darryl breathed a sigh of relief, he slowly made his way upstairs to our bedroom. He was so exhausted from the beast chasing him that he had to lay down to rest. As he tried to catch his breath, Darryl heard a noise in the backyard that sounded like horse hooves stomping, but the sound became louder and louder. Darryl was perplexed about the sound because it was getting closer. And to his surprise, he looked out our bedroom window, and the demonic horse was climbing up the wall and coming after him. As the beast got closer to the window, it neighed wickedly loud and put its head through the window and tried to take a bite out of Darryl. My brother became angry instead of terrified and, as hard as hard he could, kicked the horse in its head. The horse gave out a loud, wicked neigh, and it fell two floors to the ground. The thing ran off in a panic, and we never saw it again.

Chapter 8

I continued to battle against evil within our house in 1974. One night, I encountered the creature that I thought was long since dead since I hadn't seen it in about four years. The encounter came when I was locking up our house. Sure enough, someone left the basement light on at the rear of the basement again, and the light at the front of the basement was blown out. Before I made my way to the kitchen, I turned on the two lamps in the living room and the chandelier light that was in the dining room. As I got to the end of the dining room, I became even more fearful, and instead of going right into the kitchen, I reached my left arm around the wall and tried to feel for the kitchen light switch on the wall to turn the light on, but the kitchen light had blown out as well. Why was I surprised? Now I had to go directly to the rear of the basement with no kitchen light for illumination to turn off the only light there was between the basement and the dining room. I crept down the basement stairs with my eyes widened as big as saucers. And as soon as I turned off the only working basement light by pulling the little chain that dangled from the light fixture of the wood-studded ceiling, I ran as fast as I could in the pitch darkness, hoping I would not stumble or run into anything. I become so utterly terrified that I could have jumped right out of my skin. The spiky black-haired beast growled very angrily and chased me up to the basement stairs to the kitchen, through the dining room to the living room, then to the stairs that led to the second floor (where it never came).

I yelled, "Mommy! Mommy! Help me!"

My mother (Gina) immediately jumped out of bed and ran to meet me on the stairs. The monster reached for me, and quickly, I was in its grasp, but it saw my mother. It growled and stared at her, and she stared at it. My mother yelled very loudly for the thing to leave me alone, along with belting out some spiritual and exorcising words, and it froze dead in its tracks.

"Leave my son alone and go back to hell where you came from, in the name of Jesus!" my mother bellowed.

The evil thing ceased grabbing me and quickly slithered back into the basement, where it soon vanished for some time. That night, I found comfort within my mother's embrace, sleeping right beside her for the duration of that night. She assured me that she would never allow any harm to come to me, but I kept peering at the black iron railing and the banister of the stairwell, thinking that the creature just might finally get the nerve to come upstairs and make its attack. At this time, I felt like less of a man to be afraid of monsters as I was approaching age sixteen and decided to confront the beast head on and destroy it.

Chapter 9

The war in Vietnam was finally over, and I missed going to that war by just a couple of years. My mother was sure relieved. She never wanted me to go or any of my younger brothers. Often we heard bad news about my mother's friends' sons or some of our neighbors' sons who had gotten killed or returned awfully maimed. There was an awful lot of sobbing at my home during those years when my mother's sisters and friends visited. I wasn't afraid to join the service. I was just so opposed to the Vietnam War. It didn't make any sense to me—although most wars seldom make any sense to me, except World War II and some of the biblical battles that took place. I watched a lot of news for a young teen, so I usually had war on my mind. Even one of my friends and I used to talk about the threat of nuclear war with Russia while sitting on the top of his garage, which frightened us a lot. I really felt that war with the Soviets was inevitable. And my favorite reporters were Walter Cronkite and Philadelphia's John Facenda. When I watched them report, I watched intensively. I was in awe. They were so intelligent, profound, and dedicated getting the news to the people of America, and they seemed to stand for good.

In 1976, after high school graduation, I wanted to go to college to become a reporter or politician. I didn't get any help from my high school counselor at Camden High or from the college recruiter at Rutgers University Camden, who said I was not college material. His advice to my mother was for me to join the rest of the blue-collar community in the workforce. And that's when I became interested in joining the US Air Force. My father was in the air force during the Korean War. My grandfather (my mother's father) was in World War I and was in the big parade in New York City when the troops returned from Europe. One of my mother's older brothers was in World War II in the US Marines and fought against Hitler and Mussolini soldiers in North Africa. He had been severely shell-shocked and then released.

I didn't go to college right away because I initially believed what the college recruiter had told me. So one day, I went to the local air force recruiting office in Philadelphia. I started asking some questions.

The office personnel stared at me and the way I was dressed, which was with big bell-bottoms, platform shoes,

Coke-bottle eyeglasses with very thick lenses, and a Jackson 5 Afro hairstyle. They paused, looked at each other, and then burst out laughing.

"You want to join what, son?" one of them asked jokingly.

They laughed at me so hard that they laughed me right out of the building with my head hanging downward. My eyeglasses were pretty thick. And I knew my chances for joining the air force were over. I never thought about joining any of the other branches of the armed forces at that time, so I started focusing on college a little bit harder.

Shortly thereafter, I started having war-type dreams. One dream took me to a futuristic Nazi America. It was similar to the Nazi Germany of the 1930s and 1940s, but it was right here in the good old "US of A." Adolf Hitler was resurrected from the grave by the devil. He amassed a great army and took over most of the world. I tried to evade Hitler's "Third Reich," which was quickly reassembled after his resurrection. I was crawling in tunnels and small spaces. The Nazi army prevailed against what seemed to be a nonexisting military in the United States, until the Chinese military arrived. They arrived unannounced and uninvited. They came onto our shores just like we did on the shores of Normandy on "D-day" of World War II. They quickly scoured the United States looking for the Nazi military.

During this time, the Nazi army turned their attention from fighting the few Americans that hadn't gone underground and were still on the surface to fighting the Chinese army. The Chinese had a huge and superior military. They quickly prevailed against Hitler and the Nazi military. It was very strange observing this war that they were fighting in the United States. I was happy that the Chinese were beating the Nazi army; however, I was also extremely afraid of them because of the size of their military and the technical advancement their weaponry. They were a lot more mysterious than any country I could imagine. I had no hate for them at all. But I hated the Nazi army. I was willing to fight them if I had to because I was extremely angry with them for their arrogance and how they tried to take over the world and the tactics they used to do it and for the mere fact that they thought everyone was beneath them. The Chinese never angered me, but I was awfully afraid of their numbers. I always knew that their military would consist of billions of soldiers. Just thinking about how a small part of their military can outnumber our entire population was staggering.

The Chinese soon backed the Nazi military into retreat all over the United States. The Chinese were everywhere, although they posed no threat to Americans. They never demanded anything nor exercised any force against us. They were just present, almost like guardians. And we stayed out of their way. They obliterated the Nazi military, and their few remnants were forced to leave the United

States. The Chinese also left without saying a word. As for the Americans, those of us who survived the onslaught of Hitler's "Third Reich" came out of hiding. America seemed uninhabited, as if everyone had lived in caves. I could only compare it to H. G. Wells's *War of the Worlds*. Only this time there were two types of aliens: the Nazis and the Chinese, one extremely evil and one good.

Chapter 10

As I grew into a man, monsters were pretty much a thing of the past; however, there was one last encounter from the creature in the basement at our home in Camden. As I went to lock up one night, while approaching the basement, a devilish red beast jumped out. All these years, I had only been accustomed with the hairy black beast from previous torments, but this thing had the mannerisms of the first beast. It was as if the previous creature had transformed itself into this because they were the same in stature and shaped exactly the same. This thing had devil horns sticking out of its forehead. Its face was hideously disfigured, and it smelled like a large bag of assholes. It chased me from the kitchen through the dining room to the living room. Again, I was moving in slow motion, and time seemed to stand still. And from behind me it said horridly, "I want your soul, Danny. I want your soul. And I shall have it! There's nothing you can do. There's nothing anyone can do. You're mine now."

The evil creature wanted to destroy me. As I reached for the banister and tried to get upstairs, the creature put a spell on me, causing me to freeze in my tracks. I could not move as the devil-like beast glared at me. It taunted me and looked me over with its sharp, pointy claws as if it were to going to feast on me. But my mind and my mouth were not frozen. This time I didn't yell for my mother. I called on Jesus, the Creator of all things.

"Jesus!" I exclaimed.

My voice crescendoed and bounced off the walls of our house. Jesus appeared between me and the monster. The expression on the beast's face was inexplicable. The monster was wide-eyed and had its mouth wide open when Jesus, in all of his glory, appeared. He slew the creature with the words of his mouth. And his tongue looked like it was a two-edged sword. And he destroyed the monster right in front of me. And it was utterly destroyed; nothing remained of it.

Some time had passed, and I was now twenty and had outgrown my boyhood bedroom. There had been four of us occupying one little room, and my younger brothers were getting bigger, and since I was the eldest, I figured it should be me that left the room and found somewhere else to sleep. So I slept downstairs on the living room couch.

One night, I was sleeping soundly, and all of a sudden I heard a lion's roar. At first, the sound was off at a distance, but it kept getting louder and louder until the sound was right at my ear. I often read the Holy Bible, and I remembered where God stated, "The devil, our adversary, roams about like a roaring lion, seeking whom he may devour." Instantly, I made the analogy and cried out for Jesus, and he protected me. The lion's roaring ceased, and again, I was at peace.

As I got into my midtwenties, my dreams had become more apocalyptic in nature. It was of a construct of stuff that hadn't happened yet but was soon going to happen due to the prophecies of the great prophets of old.

I had moved from my childhood home in Camden northward to New Brunswick and Piscataway, New Jersey, where I went to college at Rutgers, beginning in January 1983, after transferring from Camden County College in Blackwood one semester shy of an associate's degree. This was my first time experiencing dreams outside my normal environment.

One hot summer night, when the sky was clear and the constellation was vivid and illuminating, I stood on my back, stooped, and gazed up into the sky and saw something

I had never seen before. It looked like a star, but it was not. Its shape was that of a burst and consisted of magnificent colors: purple, red, blue, and green. The star had great movement, unlike normal stars, and approached me. A spirit projected himself to me, letting me know that he was the ultimate power and would be returning in like manner as the apostles of old had seen him go, which was in the sky and not descending to earth (not touching the ground). And I smiled at the magnificent star and was reassured of his return in the near future. From that point, I was transported through time and space and wound up in Saudi Arabia— no black holes or portholes just by some entity's sheer will. Whose will? I didn't have the slightest clue. All I knew is that I was in a land where many structures resembled the Taj Mahal.

To my dismay, when examining the architecture, I heard ruffling sounds in the trees that surrounded one of the buildings, only to hear sounds of tigers on the prowl. The tigers had sensed that I was in the area and came after me. At first, I didn't see any tigers when I was outside the building, but I wasn't going to wait around to see them, so I immediately hurried to the front door and tried to get inside the building to get out of harm's way, with no way of knowing what I would find inside. For all I knew, the structure could have been swarming with other tigers on the inside as well, but that was a chance I had to take.

"Great! The door's not locked," I said to myself. Immediately, I went inside. It was breathtaking. It was indeed a palace where sultans once dwelt. One of the tigers burst into the foyer of the palace and lunged at me. Thank God, I was standing next to an extremely long and thick drapery. They hung from the extremely high ceilings, which was over fifty feet high. I climbed up the drapery as quickly as I could, and the tiger tried to follow, but it couldn't because its claws were too sharp, which cut through the drapery like butter on its first jump. It made several attempts to jump as high as it could, getting the same result. The tiger kept sliding down the drapery back to the glassy floor of the palace. The tiger was really pissed off now, but it just glared up at me and waited pacing back and forth, licking its chops. However, I found another way out without coming back down the drapery. I climbed all the way to the very top of the drapery and found a tight opening in the wall, just enough for my body to fit through. The opening led to tunnels in the building. The tunnel I chose lead downward and into the garden surrounding the estate. I cautiously crawled out of the small space into the garden unbeknownst to what I would find. But I didn't see or hear any tigers.

"Thank God," I said to myself.

I never once saw any people. I supposed that the tigers ate them all, which would explain the bones I saw in the garden. So I escaped near death by the skin of my teeth.

Chapter 11

On occasion, I would fall into a very deep sleep, or as some would call it, "dreams within dreams." Sometimes I fell into second and third levels of subconscious dreams, which were extremely difficult to come out of to return to reality or the original level of subconsciousness.

"Here I am in these damn fields again! How in the hell do I keep ending up here?" I said out loud.

I was so pissed off. I just started walking. I didn't pause or look in each direction to try to contemplate which way would be the bleakest as I normally did. I didn't care about which direction I should go in anymore. I got so sick and tired of trying to figure out which direction would be the one that would be disastrous or not, like I had done in the past. And as I had always known, there was seldom a pleasant environment or experience.

Once again, after a pretty lengthy walk, I walked into a town that resembled my childhood city to the teeth (Camden, New Jersey). I went to the house that looked like mine and knocked on the door. The door swung open, and one of my brothers was there. It was Darryl.

"Hi, Darryl!" I exclaimed.

"Hello, Danny!" my brother said.

"Darryl, what are you doing in my dream?" I asked.

"I don't know! How do you know you're not in my dream?" Darryl retorted.

I didn't respond. I just looked at him as if he was crazy. He told me that there was some strange goings-on lately.

"Darryl, you know what your problem is? You stay in the house too much. You need to get some fresh air," I said.

"You know I'm not the outdoor sort of guy," Darryl replied.

"I'm going outside. It's stuffy in the house," I said.

I just hung out on the front stoop. Then, I walked out onto the lawn, and a strange looking giant black hand (from out of nowhere) tried to grab me. I managed to elude the demonic hand's grasp and hurriedly ran back into the house where it did not follow.

"Darryl!" "Darryl!" "You're not going to believe what I just saw!" I said.

"What did you see, Danny?" Darryl said sarcastically.

"A giant black hand came from out of nowhere and tried to grab me and squeeze me to a pulp!" "It swiped at me while closing to a fist." I said.

"Are you feeling well, Danny?" Darryl said jokingly.

"I'm feeling fine." "You don't believe me do you?" I said.

"Danny just calm down and have something to eat." "How about some raisin brand cereal?" He said.

"Raisin brand cereal?" "Now Darryl, I know you have some meat around here somewhere!" "You always have some meat." "We don't call you meat head for nothing unless you're trying to keep it all for yourself." I said gloatingly.

"No Danny really!" "All we have is raisin brand cereal." Darryl said.

"Ha ha ha!" "You're real funny Danny." Darryl said.

So I made myself a bowl of raisin brand cereal until I was able to get to a store later that night to get some meat. Then someone knocked at the door. I went to the door, opened it and stuck my head out to see who it was. I saw nothing. With the bowl of cereal in my hand, I stepped out on the front stoop then down to the lawn.

Then down to the front lawn, the black giant hand darted toward me. I panicked and fell down. The bowl of Raisin Bran cereal flung into the air in the direction of the giant hand. The hand froze for a second and ceased attacking me. But I couldn't, for the life of me, figure out why.

"This doesn't make any sense! What in the world could it be that repelled the giant grotesque hand? The last encounter, it wanted to pulverize me and squeeze me to a pulp, and now it whimpers away like a scared puppy. What's different about me now than the first time? I know! I didn't have the bowl of cereal," I said to myself.

The next morning, I went outside, bright and early, looking for the mysterious hand. I was truly unafraid, seeing how it cowered the day before. I waited and waited, but the hand did not appear. I walked up and down the ten hundred block of Kenwood Avenue. Then I gave up looking and proceeded back to the front yard of my house. As I entered my front gate, the hand mysteriously appeared above the rooftop of the row homes where I lived. It hovered over the corner house just near the intersection where Kenwood Avenue and Walnut Street met. It just so happened that I had a small box of raisins in my pocket. I took one of the raisins out and held it between my index finger and my thumb. And as the hand swooped down to me, it saw the raisin, but too late and realized what I was holding in my hand. But it was on me. It reacted toward the raisin as if it were kryptonite to Superman. The hand came within inches of me, and then *poof!* It vanished for good. I stood there perplexed and said to myself, "What in the hell just happened here and what was that all about? I'd better stop eating those pork sausages late at night. It's causing me to see things even during the day."

Chapter 12

Among the many journeys in mind, I ventured back to one of my childhood churches, St. Bartholomew's Catholic Church in Camden, New Jersey. The other church was St. Peter and Paul's Catholic Church, which was several blocks away from St. Bart's and was attached to the parochial school I attended from first to fourth grade. St. Bart's, at one time, also had a school attached to it. But there had been a fire that burned down the school a year prior to me entering the first grade. My older sister Lana and my older cousins (the Wades) attended the school for years. And I so wanted to attend also, but that would never happen because of the fire. Since St. Bart's was our original church/school, we continued attending Mass there and not St. Peter and Paul's. In fact, most of the families who had children attending St. Peter and Paul's for school attended St. Bartholomew's for church on Sunday because we were loyal and had attended for so many years. Other people we didn't know attended St. Peter and Paul's for church.

On one particular dreary and cloudy day in 1975, I walked from Parkside to what the locals called Crosstown. It was a three-mile walk from Kaighn and Haddon avenues to Kaighn and Broadway, which were the largest and main streets in Camden, New Jersey. Crosstown was in between Parkside and South Camden. During my walk, I made a stop at my old church (St. Bartholomew) on Kaighn Avenue, which I was sort of fond of.

As I was walked through the doors of the church, an extremely dark and gloomy presence set over the church and inside as well. The landscape behind the church had made a strange transformation. In its normal setting, the church was surrounded by houses and stores. But there wasn't anything normal about what I visualized. After working my way to the rear of the church, I walked through a small door, which led me to the backyard. The houses and stores that were once there were now gone. They had just vanished.

Shortly after entering the backyard of the church, it suddenly appeared as if it were night, and there was an ocean—as boisterous and tumultuous as seas become. This was an eerie sight but not as eerie as what I saw coming out of the sea. I felt like St. John on the island of Patmos when he was shown symbolic visions by Jesus Christ that represented futuristic events that were to come upon the earth. I stood paralyzed when I saw an illuminating white skull with crossbones emerge from the sea behind the church. I was no longer in shock about the sea being there behind the church, in the middle of the city where there should only have been dry land. But I was now horrified by this thing. The skull floated in my direction, which had a grimace on its bony face. I came out of my paralysis and ran as fast as I could, but the skull stayed on my tail. Gasping for air, I ran for several blocks all the way back down Kaighn Avenue toward Parkside, almost in the opposite direction from whence I had come. I finally arrived at the intersection of Kaighn and Haddon. I was getting closer to my home. I somehow lost the hellish skull by making a quick left turn at that intersection. At least, I thought I did.

Haddon Avenue was one of the busier streets, unlike Kaighn Avenue, which hardly had any activity.

Many people were moving about. I remained on the busiest sections of this street for a while. The glowing evil skull did not follow me onto this street, which was not as old and scary- looking as Kaighn Avenue where there were hardly any passersby. And unbeknownst to me, the skull had waited for me to get to the next street (Wildwood Avenue, which was very narrow) and the street I usually turned down that eventually led me to my house. It was very dark and unfriendly looking.

"How long will I have to wait?" I asked myself.

Eventually, I had to go home. I knew I couldn't wait on Haddon Avenue forever because the longer I waited, there would be less people traveling back and forth, and I would be putting my life in greater danger. I was contemplating this when I peered down Wildwood Avenue. I couldn't continue on Haddon Avenue in the direction toward my home because it was totally dead going that way, and there was an old cemetery to the left across from Walnut Avenue, which was the small cobblestoned street my street intersected. There was a bar on the right, on corner of Haddon and Walnut, which was dark and gloomy on the inside, but it hardly ever had any patrons.

There was no way I was going in that direction. So I had to go through some of the darkest residential parts of Wildwood Avenue to get home, which was in a part of Parkside that was engrossed in darkness. Even during the day, most streets were dark because of all the trees.

So I cautiously crept down Wildwood Avenue from Haddon, keeping my body close to the buildings. I never walked out in the open or down the middle of the street. I tried very desperately to get to my street (Kenwood Avenue), which was another two blocks over and two blocks down, for I lived on the ten hundred block where Kenwood began.

As cautious as I was, the skull had outmaneuvered me. It was once back on my tail when no passersby in sight. The skull from hell tried to end my life this night by viciously ripping into my neck. I frantically beat the skull away from my neck as it managed to get a few bites from my hands. I was bleeding and terrified but glad that it didn't bite my neck. I had to retreat to Haddon Avenue, which was a block behind me, but a few people were still walking about. The skull refrained from its attack and vanished. I did not proceed home but felt a need to go back in the other direction.

As I walked back to Haddon Avenue then Kaighn Avenue, I was compelled to head back toward the church even though it was several blocks away. However, I avoided getting too close to the church. So I diverted southwest of that area and wandered into the part of the city where I saw what looked like a humongous isolated and abandoned warehouse. There were no other buildings or anything around it for blocks. It just stood off at a distance as an eyesore—a freakish-looking monstrosity, if you will, emerged. It kind of reminded me of the lighthouses I saw in the "fields" and how they stood off at a distance. However, they were beautiful structures. But there was nothing beautiful about this grotesque building. It was huge and square with large black-stained windows. Its color was dingy tan and gray. It was very old and appeared to be constructed in the 1920s or earlier.

Unbeknownst to me, there was an ocean behind this monstrous structure, just like there was behind the church. This building and the church were only about three miles from each other. Ironically, the church was in town, and the very large building was on the outskirts of town near Highway 676 that led to the suburbs.

I was fascinated that there were, now, two oceans in the same city connected by the Delaware River—one ocean on the east of town and the other to the south. This made no sense to me geographically, but I did visualize it.

As I ventured toward the isolated structure, the glowing evil skull with crossbones appeared. Again, I ran for my life. The skull was on my tail once more. I knew I could not stop running until I could get to safety. I made my way from Crosstown to Parkside again. I was just a step ahead of the illuminating skull. I ran about three miles without stopping and managed to get back to Haddon Avenue where there were people and where the skull seemingly never followed. But this time, the skull tricked me. It ascended high above the city. No one saw it but me. I didn't say anything to anyone about the skull. I didn't want them to think I was crazy and clear away from me. Anyway, I stopped running when I came to the intersection of Haddon and Kaighn. I squatted down and leaned against the wall of the closed drugstore, which was on this corner, and tried to catch my breath. I staggered down Haddon Avenue until I came to Wildwood for the second time that night. Exhausted and weary yet again, I was only a few blocks from home. Once more, regardless of the dim streetlights, I acknowledged how dark this street really was. This time, I wasn't compelled to go anywhere but home. I wasn't as confused as before when I had made a beeline right back to where I started. I stopped at the intersection of the eleven-hundred block of Princess and Wildwood. There was a corner store there, and they were just getting ready to close. There were a few people patronizing the store. I didn't go in. I no longer looked at the passersby as my protection for I was now getting mad. I made my way down the eleven hundred block of Princess Avenue to the next intersection. The skull caught up to me, trying to terrorize me out of my mind. I was terribly winded. I really didn't feel like running anymore. I struggled running down the street. I saw a baseball mitt and bat some kid must have left on his porch.

With unfound energy, I leaped up onto the porch and grabbed the bat. The skull was now hovering at the intersection of Princess and Wildwood with the worst glowing evil grimace staring straight at me. The store was closed, and there was absolutely no one on the streets. I proceeded back toward the skull with bat in hand and mad as hell. The skull seemingly catapulted itself toward me then made circles around me making an awful squealing sound. It looked down at my hand to see what was in it and started laughing at me. Then it stopped circling and was now facing me at about fifteen feet away. It lunged at me and opened its mouth intermittently clamping down, viciously trying to bite me. I swung the bat with all the might I could muster and made contact with the evil skull and crossbones. The sheer power of my swing plus my anger and the will of my mind obliterated the skull into dust. I pulverized the skull, and it was no more.

Chapter 13

The 1970s had passed, and the 1980s ushered in giving me newfound responsibilities. I was now a grown man with a wife, a child, and a college degree that were forthcoming. I also had renewed my faith in Christ with a new seriousness and tried to share my convictions with everyone I personally came in contact, especially my family. My dreams drifted toward a realm of spirituality. And on one occasion, I was carried to the Middle East where holy men purged themselves for want of salvation, purification, and redemption.

Mecca was the destination for most, but it could not be obtained until some purging took place. That's when I materialized in a small, old beaten-up village where poverty had gotten the better of the villagers, and almost all of them seemed lost and afraid—having no future, no past, and wandering around aimlessly without hope.

My trek first began in Egypt, where the surroundings were pleasant and untouched by time or modern human construction. Everything was orderly. Nothing seemed out of place except one thing. The town appeared to be uninhabited. I did not see one solitary soul. So I ventured eastward to Saudi Arabia. I started to see people. I ran into a little boy and said to him, "Hello! Do you speak English?"

The boy just stood there gazing at me. I repeated my question to the dirty little boy, "I said, 'Do you speak English?'"

The boy ran away from me. And about five minutes later, two men with semiautomatic rifles walked toward me. I was startled and immediately raised my arms to indicate that I didn't want any trouble.

One of the men said, "So, you're American?" in a thick accent.

"Yes," I replied.

"What in the hell are you doing here?" said the other man that was with him.

"I'm going to see the king," I said.

"King?" said the native Arabian. "You're an American, and you're searching for your king here?"

"Yes," I retorted. "My king is the king of all. He's the king of the universe," I gracefully replied.

The Arabian then asked, "What is your king's name?"

And I told him, "His name is Jesus."

"Jesus?" said the Arabian. "We have heard of this Jesus you mentioned, but he was just a man, no?"

"He is not just a man! He is king of kings and of the universe, as I told you before," I said to the man.

Then the Arabian asked me, "Where is this Jesus? I don't see him! I've only heard stories!"

"What man would die for the sins of the world? What fantasy!" he said.

I responded, "It's true! He did die on the cross for the sins of the world. And his kingdom shall have no end."

The Arabian then said, "How do you know this? Where have you gotten this information, my American friend?"

I replied, "It's in his Word, and he has revealed his word to my mind."

The Arabian laughed.

"To your mind? What kind of nonsense is that? Allah makes more sense than that," replied the Arabian.

"Be on your way, and take your mind with you," he said firmly.

So I continued eastward, through the desert sand and through the eerie valleys surrounded by austere mountains. I was getting a sense of the journeys that holy men of old had traveled, succumbing to the bitter embrace of loneliness and hunger. The valley narrowed to a small dusty road, which seemed as if it had no end. My trek was interrupted by several strange people. It was as if they were placed in my path to thwart my journey. I never completed this pilgrimage, for I was mysteriously transported back to New Jersey. I felt like I had gotten the closest I would ever get to a spiritual climax in life before I was snatched out of thin air.

Chapter 14

It seemed like I had gotten back to reality. But what was that really? My second son had been born, and now Danny Jr. had a little brother. My wife, Fay, was ecstatic. It had been almost seven years between sons, but after Demetrius was born, waiting all those long years didn't matter anymore. I loved my family more than anything. I was very protective of them.

One night, at our home in Kingwood, Texas, there was a very bad thunderstorm. The lightning was out of control. The lightning kept getting closer and closer to our home. There was a moment of silence.

Then there was a loud, crackling sound seemingly at my bedroom window. The sky had brightened as if it were morning and lingered for about an hour. I had never seen anything like this before. I thought that the loud, crackling sound was thunder or lightning actually striking objects, but it was made by a gigantic stone hurling downward from the sky. The enormous rock was shaped like a cone or spinning similar to the ones I used to play with as a child, only it was bigger than a house. It was gyrating at tremendously fast revolutions. The closer it got to the earth, the sounds altered into what sounded like a loud, metallic whining sound like a large table saw, only amplified. As it hurled downward from the sky, the colossal stone gyrated into the ground at our nearby park, off the greenbelt at our subdivision in Mills Branch. It created a great chasm in the ground. It never stopped spinning. While the stone was yet spinning, and unbeknownst to me, my son Demetrius had been sleepwalking outside and walking to that very park in our neighborhood where the stone had landed. Demetrius, or Dex, as my wife and I nicknamed him, had been gazing at the stone the entire time it had been descending from the sky. He was so fascinated that it was as if he were a deer caught in a vehicle's headlights. As the stone landed, it nearly hit Dex. It was as if he were in a trance, not knowing the danger he was encountering. He stood paralyzed, watching the mammoth rock drill downward into the earth.

The loud crackling sound had awakened my wife, Fay, and I but not Danny Jr. I ran to the greenbelt when I did not see Dex in the front yard or backyard of our home. When I failed to see Dex on the greenbelt, I immediately thought about the park where all little children his age like to go.

The park was about two blocks from our home. Then I saw a great hole in the ground that looked like it could swallow one or two houses. And I saw Dex standing at the edge of the precipice, nearly falling in and still in his awestruck state. I immediately yelled, "Dex! Dex!"

Dex remained there, starstruck and unable to move. I yelled for him again.

"Dex! Dex! Stop! Stop! Don't move!"

I managed to grab Dex in the nick of time before he fell into the endless chasm. The sound of the monstrous rock was soon gone. I could only imagine that the rock would either erode from its vicious cycles or be obliterated by the magma from the Earth's core.

"Dex, you all right?" I asked.

"Yes, Dad," he replied.

And as he had awakened from his sleepwalking trance. Fay and I paid careful attention to him.

Chapter 15

In the course of my adulthood dreams, I could not keep from returning to my childhood home in Camden, New Jersey, on several occasions. On one of my narcoleptic journeys, I occupied my childhood home as an adult and lived there with my wife. Even though in reality I had two boys, they were not in existence in this setting, nor were my mother, sisters, and two of my brothers there, except for Paul. Our home, in reality, was not even in this town. My mind did not include any of the realities of the true scenarios.

One night, an ex-girlfriend, named Myra, from my past was getting dressed for a night out on the town in our house. I didn't know how she got in our house. She was still under the impression that we were together, and she acted like she was totally oblivious that I was married to someone else. As she continued to dress herself in our small bathroom, with one tiny vanity, she was humming a tune and started to put on makeup. I noticed a freakish transformation happening to her. But she didn't notice anything even being right in front of the bathroom mirror. She just kept humming a tune and was acting really happy about going out. She kept putting her makeup on as if everything was normal. But I can tell you, everything was pretty freaking far from normal. I saw her morph into a hideous creature, which was very hairy from the neck up, including her arms. I tried extremely hard to act like I didn't notice the transformation. Now I had two problems: not only did she not realize I was no longer her boyfriend from nine years prior, she also didn't realize that she was a monster. So I just started having a regular conversation with her, and I told her that I would wait downstairs and watch some television. The Philadelphia 76ers was playing the Los Angeles Lakers. And no sooner than I turned the TV on, I heard a rap on the door. It was my little brother Paul.

"Hi, Paul, how are you doing?" I asked.

"Okay, Danny!" Paul replied.

"Hey, listen, Paul, what I am about to tell you is weird. I don't want you to be alarmed," I nervously and quietly said to him.

"Well, what is it, Danny?" Paul retorted like he had some place to be.

"Someone or something is upstairs, and she's turning into some kind of beast. I think it—I mean she's turning into a werewolf. First, it looked like Myra. You know, the girl I sort of dated when I was fourteen, who lived right here on our street. But the catch is, it is acting like the transformation isn't even happening. Now, I want you to act completely normal. Okay?" I quietly said to him.

"Okay, Danny!" Paul responded.

Paul and I had a longtime pact just like my wife, Fay, and I had that we would believe each other no matter how crazy something sounded. I was scared to death of what this thing had become and didn't know when it would start acting like the creature that it was. I was thinking about all kind of crazy scenarios that could ultimately lead to my death and the death of my little brother—like what if it just started its period or was going through menopause, being the monster that it was. It would probably rip my head off with little effort. I was trembling inside, but I couldn't let it see my fear.

"Now, Paul, I want us to sit down here and act like we're enjoying the game while I figure out how we can get out of here without her knowing," I said to him.

"We need to turn the volume up on the TV and make the usual sounds we normally make when we're really watching a game," Paul said.

"Now, I want you to quietly go outside and start up your car while I pretend that we are having a conversation about the basketball game. It's a good thing we sound alike so I can do both parts of the conversation. I'll increase the volume. There's no telling when it will realize what it has become and then freak out. We have no idea how it will react. And I don't want to be around when it does finally see how hideous it really is. It may rip us apart, being a werewolf and all. I'll meet you outside as soon as I get the chance," I said to Paul.

So Paul crept outside through the front door and got in his car, fearfully waiting for me. I pretended I was talking to him while the creature was still upstairs prepping itself in the bathroom, putting on its makeup and still not realizing what it looked like.

"Paul, did you see that? Dr. J just dunked on that guy as if he wasn't there!" I said out loud.

I raised the volume a little more as I sneaked out the front door and into Paul's car. Paul took his foot off the brake and slowly pushed down on the accelerator and turned left at the corner of the street, Kenwood and Walnut Streets.

I told Paul that I just wanted to get a few blocks away and that we should separate to keep him from being in danger by being with me. Paul had never seen the monster that night, when it was Myra or when it had turned into the creature. And I had only assumed that it heard Paul and I talking downstairs or heard Paul's knocking at the front door when he first came over. It may not have heard any of it. It may not have reacted like I feared it would after it saw what it really looked like, but I couldn't take any chances. Even though this person has appeared as a former friend of mine from the early '70s, I knew that this was not really her but some alien being from an alien race that perhaps abducted the real Myra.

Paul dropped me off at the intersection of Princess Avenue and Park Boulevard. I told Paul to hurriedly get as far away from the city as he could, and with looks of great concern and feelings of finality, we said our good-byes.

Back at my house on Kenwood Avenue, a horrible realization was discovered, resonating in extremely high-pitched howls. The creature finally saw how it really appeared once it finished putting on its makeup. Whatever blinders it had on initially were definitely not there anymore. The loud doglike yelps crescendoed throughout the neighborhood, but not a soul came out of their houses. When I heard it, I trembled. It was loud, and I cringed. The beast started crying. Whether it was Myra or not, I did not know. It realized that it was hideous. It ran down the stairs looking for me, expecting to find me there. It couldn't find me. It looked everywhere in the house. The television was still on, and the volume was very high. It kept crying and felt awfully alone because I had left. But then it knew that I must have known that it looked this way but was hiding my true feelings and the reality of it all the entire time I was in the house.

The tears soon stopped, and the pitiful behavior turned into rage and hate. It had nothing but contempt for me, leaving it that way with no compassion. The monster wasn't going to let bygones be bygones, but it was going to hunt me down for betraying it, and it will kill me.

Along with the beast's horrible appearance, other physical attributes took form. It acquired superhuman-like strength as well as immensely strong and huge vampire-bat–like wings. No sooner than when this thing discovered its wings, it crashed through the front door of our house, taking out a chunk of the brick wall that encased it. It took off into the night air, and it was as if it knew how to use the wings all along, by some natural animal instinct.

The hurt that the creature was feeling was quickly forgotten. The part-werewolf and part-bat that was now its makeup was commonplace, and all the creature could think about is getting its claws and fangs into me who had betrayed it. If I only had been up front and honest with it instead of hiding like a coward, it would not feel the sensation to rip me apart.

Now I was a hunted man. The werewolf that used to be my ex-girlfriend was coming after me for blood. I befriended the dark of night as I hid behind trees and vehicles. And suddenly I noticed a large image flying in the midst. The pale moonlight gave a glimpse of the colossal creature in flight, seemingly soaring in the clouds. However, it was having a difficult time spotting me because Parkside had so many trees, which turned out to be my saving grace. There were some passersby walking down Princess Avenue, and all I could think about is how I had to bond with them and make myself obscure.

"If I walk with these people, it probably won't even notice me!" I said to myself.

I had no idea, until later on, that the hideous werewolf with wing could not see me for the thickness of the trees. So I was forever cautious as I could clearly see the thing flying back and forth in the midnight sky at a distance as the moon provided a little light.

As the sun began to rise, the creature gave up looking for me, for it was exhausted from the entire ordeal. It needed to rest its wings. Now, unbeknownst to the monster, I was long gone. And in time, it gave up the search for good. But I never saw my ex-girlfriend again.

Chapter 16

From out of the blue, I had tumbled into a cornfield in Nowhere, USA. It must have been somewhere in Mississippi or Alabama because not very far from the cornfield, I saw some country bumpkins fooling around with what looked like an old-fashioned distillery. I dared not make a sound. For all I knew, my carelessness could cause me to be dangling from the end of a rope. Well, it didn't look quite like the old south that I pictured, and I couldn't have been any more careful than I already was. I fathomed that I would never escape on foot because I had no idea where I was. I tried my best to be as obscure as possible. I hid myself very well that night and ended up underneath a bunch of rubbish in the back of an old pickup.

Later that night, the owner of the truck I was hiding in got in and started the engine. The truck was very old and beaten but ran fairly well. The truck had an awful light blue color and rust all over it. The man had referred to himself in the first person. His name was Earl, and he kept saying he had a taste for some corn liquor, so he headed over to his friend's shack. His friend's name was Beauregard, and supposedly Beauregard always had corn liquor around.

As Earl was driving down the dark country roads, I was getting annoyed and antsy because Earl kept talking to himself about going to Beauregard's and how he couldn't wait to get his mitts on his liquor.

"I can't wait! Earl can't wait! Beauregard's liquor goes down so smooth I want to drink a gallon of it," he kept saying to himself with his country twang.

"Damn hick," I said to myself. I had no idea where I was. I didn't know whether I should jump out of Earl's truck while he was driving down the dark back roads or wait until he came to a place I recognized. I peeked my head out of the pickup and saw an old filling station that sure seemed familiar. I had remembered seeing that same road that led to the filling station, but I just couldn't remember when. I figured if I was ever going to flee this town, there would be no better time for me to do it than the present. So I climbed out of the truck when Earl slowed down to make a left turn. I jumped over some brush, seeing that that he had slowed down to about ten miles an hour to make the turn. Undetected by the hillbilly, I ducked down as low as I could in the brush and slowly started walking down that road. I walked for hours undetected. I ended up in a place where I felt a little safer. So I escaped another near tragic ending.

Chapter 17

My mind was spiraling out of control as I ended up in my childhood neighborhood again through a mental porthole of some sort. This time, forensic police were hunting down a vicious killer and looking for leads and possible suspects in a murder that happened in New Jersey. As I tried to figure out why the police were looking so fervently, it dawned on me that I remembered standing over a dead body while holding a revolver in my hand.

"I must have killed somebody! But I can't, for the life of me, figure out why or who," I said to myself.

Patrol cars swarmed my neighborhood like locusts; however, I managed to evade them. Later, I remembered that I had used a pick and shovel for something. It was like I was coming out of a trance.

"I couldn't have murdered someone, could I? It's not like me, but all of the evidence points to me. Where's the body?" I asked myself.

As I scurried about in my basement in the dark, I bumped into a rolled-up carpet.

"I don't remember this being here! Someone must be playing a trick on me!" I said.

Inside the carpet was a dead body, some young African American male that I didn't know. I was now thoroughly convinced that I had killed someone. But maybe I wasn't myself when I did it. My first instinct was to bury the body before it started to decompose or before someone discovered it.

That night, I quickly transported the body to the trunk of my car that was parked in the alley behind my house. I had driven to an old abandoned granite mine in Pennsylvania. I carefully buried the body deep into the granite all the way to the back of the mine. Also, I made sure that I buried the gun.

Months past, and I was still apprehensive. There was a little part of me that felt I didn't commit the murder and that I was being set up. I didn't want to confess to the police because I wasn't 100 percent sure that I was not guilty.

A year had passed, and the police had pretty much given up the search for the murderer and the missing body, or so I thought. I was still very nervous because after a year had gone by and with the police seemingly closing the case, some hotshot detective made one last massive effort to conduct an intensive manhunt, which brought them around to my neighborhood again.

Eventually, I was questioned, but it was more of an interrogation. The detective had asked me to account for all of the places I had been and what I had done. This was a year after the initial investigation.

"You expect me to remember and account for each and every place I've been, and it's been over a year? You guys are pathetic!" I said to him.

Detective Bertolli stared at me for a couple of seconds.

"Mister, you may think we're beating a dead horse, but we tend to think we know what we're doing!" he exclaimed.

I just looked at the detective with a cynical look on my face.

"Okay, do what you gotta do," I said.

The detective had some forensic police comb through my home from top to bottom. I feared that something would be discovered. But nothing was. Many months had passed, then years. Nothing was discovered. At least, for now!

Chapter 18

The year was 1993. My wife materialized right in front of me after being gone for three years. She said that she had been with some strange beings in a strange place, but they were pretty good to her, so she didn't panic too much. However, they ran a lot of tests on her. They, especially, wanted to find out how her brain worked. She said that she went through several lobotomies, in which she was awake when they conducted them. She didn't experience any pain because these beings had a technology far superior to ours. I didn't mention to her about how the aliens had left a being on Earth that looked like her and the ordeal I had experienced. I didn't want to go into that. I figured she had gone through enough already. I just told her about how I took care of Danny Jr. in her absence and some of the things we did. Danny Jr. was ecstatic to see her.

One night in 1995, I subconsciously hurled into a realm of sleep that foreshadowed some of the nuances of my life. We lived in Maple Shade, New Jersey, just outside of Philadelphia, a quaint little spot. However, the amount we had to pay for rent was astronomical—even for a two-bedroom apartment. I knew we couldn't keep going on at this rate, so I had to find a higher paying job. The salary that I earned as an administrative for Con Air's Chief Pilots Office was nearly enough to feed my family. I had worked for the Chief Pilots Office for thirteen years and had only received a raise when I transferred from Newark to Houston. But it still wasn't enough to maintain a family of four. So I applied to become a pilot for Con Air where the salaries were somewhat conducive to the economy. Well, at least I knew my family wouldn't starve.

I already had four hundred hours of flight time on the Cessna, which I acquired on my time off at a regional airport in Pemberton, New Jersey, and received my private pilot's license. I was accepted at Con Air after I passed all four of my interviews—which were comprised of a distinguished panel of professionals from the training department, Chief Pilots Office, and Fleet Managers Office—with flying colors. I astounded the elite group of experienced pilots with my knowledge of the company's technical and aeronautical information of Con Air's aircraft. My employment in the Chief Pilots Office gave me opportunities to study flight manuals, operation manuals, as well as maps and charts.

On September 16 of 1995, I finished my six weeks of pilot training. The pilots called it "the fire hose syndrome," on account that it was like putting a fire hose in your mouth and turning the water on full blast, because the training was so intense and fast-paced. I passed the simulator, lofts, and IOE (Initial Operations Experience) training as well as my line checks (real cockpit observance by a check airman while in flight). No one that knew me was surprised that I had done so well because they knew how I excelled at anything I had put my mind to. And I already had a college degree in English and history. It wasn't uncommon for guys like me wanting to become pilots. Besides, Con Air had many pilots with degrees in various fields although there were also many that had received their flight experience in the armed forces.

Now with all of the training under my belt, it was time for me to conduct the first leg of my flight. Classified as an *MD80* First Officer, I was preparing myself for my first real full flight with Con Air. There was no doubt that I was nervous. My first flight was from Newark to Puerta Plata. I spent a lot of time going over the maps and charts in my *Jeppesen* manual. As I neared the time to get on the aircraft, I knew that I had to do a walk-around first. The *MD80* aircraft checked out okay. I then returned to the aircraft and sat in the right seat with my flight bag at my right side. However, I was still nervous. I was apprehensive about what I thought I saw on one of my maps. In my mind, I questioned the map I was looking at regarding the end of the runway in Puerta Plata. According to the map, the runway came to an abrupt end. Ostensibly, the runway appeared to look shorter than it was supposed to be. Initially, I didn't say anything to the captain or check airman. I nervously started second-guessing my abilities and all of my rigorous training about landing properly. My takeoff was cinch, but the landing?

I aced landing in the simulator. It was just something about descending. Then about three hundred miles from the approach, I explained my reluctance to the captain and the check airman, who was sitting in the cockpit jump seat.

"Danny, if you feel apprehensive about the landing, we can have the check airman land. It may not sit well with the Chief Pilot's Office, but they'll just have to reschedule you," said the captain.

"I'm sure you're right, Captain! I wouldn't feel like this if Puerta Plata had a longer runway," I said with uncertainty.

"I tell you what, Danny, you switch seats with the check airman, and you observe, okay? We've done this many times before, and the runway seems okay to us," said the captain.

"Okay, Brandon, that may be the correct thing to do," I responded, with an embarrassed tone of voice.

Capt. Brandon Aldano calmed me down. And when we reached Puerta Plata, the runway appeared totally different than the map had indicated. There was a village at the end of the runway; however, the actual huts were not positioned in the path of the runway but were at a safe distance from the wingspan of our aircraft. At the end of the runway, there was an extensive dirt road that did not appear on the map. It would not have imposed any impending danger if we did go beyond the safety barrier because the aircraft would have cleared any dangerous areas.

As the check airman, Ron Sabemoon, was on his final approach, I started to feel at ease. My confidence returned as he landed smoothly and stopped the aircraft with plenty of room to spare.

"I could have done that! I could have done this landing! It would have been a piece of cake!" I said emphatically to Brandon and Ron.

Chapter 19

In the year 2025, many technological advances were made, especially in space travel. NASA, Boeing, and Con Air merged and started the first civilian planetary travel. After many years of research and preparation, star trekking had become possible. Warp speed was now able to propel men, women, and children as far as Pluto if need be. Ergo, it was only available to billionaires and multimillionaires. The cheapest ticket was priced at $250,000,000, round trip in economy. And the costs of their quarters were made by their previous investments in NASA, Boeing, and Con Air.

During this time, Earth's geological and atmospheric condition was making our planet unsuitable for human and animal life. Those who were extremely wealthy were privy to those conditions and hurriedly purchased tickets to the planets that were conducive to their lifestyle. Just about all of the planets were more than suitable for colonization, but some were just a little bit more luxurious and pleasant than others as was shown in the brochures of the travel agencies to the filthy rich.

As Con Air beefed up its number of space shuttles to meet the demands of their clients, and being the only former air carrier to do so, NASA and Boeing put the final enhancements on the planets, their colonies, and the space shuttles.

Houston Interstellar Spaceport, renamed, was now ready to receive its first of many interstellar travelers after years of construction. Operated much like an airport, there were enormous Jetways that had the space shuttles docked to them. All baggage was brought directly to the gates, which had huge screening rooms near the gates where luggage and passengers were screened prior to boarding.

So it began: the mass exodus to the other planets in our solar system. The very rich from all over the world flocked to the spaceport in Houston while the middle classes serviced them as spaceport employees contemplating their meager existence. The rich journeyed to Mars and Venus. They trekked to Uranus and Jupiter.

While the rich were escaping their impending doom on Earth, the middle classes and the poor were moving into their lavish homes. Chaos was rampant. Those who dared secure those estates of the wealthy did it at their own risk. They had to strap themselves down with what artillery they had or could steal. Law enforcement was so corrupt that most of them had secured the finer mansions and homes for themselves because they had better access to the finer and more powerful guns. The military were no better than the police as they also muscled in on those territories left behind by the grossly affluent. The politicians that remained that weren't affluent kept trying to reason with rest of the people through media. No one was listening to them.

While total bedlam was the reality of the planet Earth, those who could afford to escape did. There weren't very many of the affluent that remained behind, except those philanthropists who had compassion for people. Some were medical doctors, nurses, and a few scientists worldwide.

As time progressed, of course, it became exceedingly worse on Earth. However, unbeknownst to the rich living comfortably on the different planets in our solar system, the scientists at NASA miscalculated the conditions of our galaxy. Oh, there was no doubt that Earth was in trouble, but the other planets, as livable as they seemed, had less longevity than Earth because Earth had a special protective shield, although damaged, that the other planets in the solar system did not have. This was an oversight never detected by the most brilliant minds in science.

The whole time the rich were away was just seven years. They had lived comfortably while most of those on Earth were suffering. Information had gotten to them by satellite that the planets in our solar system were dissolving quickly. Earth was dissolving the slowest. Some of the scientists who had remained on Earth discovered the demise of the planets through their research and had contacted their fellow scientists in space. And now there was mass hysteria among those who colonized the planets. They wanted to get back to Earth.

Now a mass exodus back to Earth was in progress. The scientists on the colonies had been made aware of how horrific the Earth had become, but there was no time or advanced technology to venture beyond our solar system. There was no choice but to go back to Earth where the millionaires, the middle classes, and the poor were fighting among themselves for survival.

As an employee for Con Air for thirty-seven years, I had witnessed many of the wealthy leave our spaceport. But after they left, the spaceport was dismantled, and all of the spaceport employees were either laid off or transferred to other existing air carriers. Con Air no longer existed. Houston went back to an intercontinental airport. We never anticipated that the wealthy were ever going to return. But they must have felt that they would someday, or they wouldn't have left everything intact as they did.

Emergency landings had to be prepared. When the space shuttles landed, they landed on whatever runways that were locked into their coordinates. ATC had airplanes diverting to small outstations to make room for the number of space shuttles to land at the large hubs.

The inception was not pretty. The rich flocked back to their mansions only to find themselves on a battleground with those who occupied their estates. Bloodshed, massive bloodshed ran rampant over Earth. Everyone was out for themselves. Those who were left behind weren't going to give up what they had attained. And the billionaires and multimillionaires wanted their land back.

They wanted all of their belongings back. But what did they expect? Did they really think for one minute everything would be hunky-dory during their return? They knowingly left everyone who couldn't afford to go on Earth to die! For seven years, the masses knew it, and they hated them for it.

The superwealthy knew they had to do something. Some of the wealthy did have hidden arsenals buried underground in various areas of their estates and some off the property. They assembled a task force comprised of all who were ex-military, FBI, CIA, DEA, and other law enforcement agencies or those who had training in firearms.

Some of the superwealthy had less difficulty than others. Those in the state of California had it the worst. Gangs had taken over some of the estates in Beverly Hills, Santa Monica, and San Diego. Those that had estates in more remote and mountainous areas still found their properties intact.

The battle between them lasted a couple of months before the wealthy could gain an advantage. Some of their mansions suffered some degradation while they were gone. Nevertheless, those in opposition were outgunned. And soon, literally all of the wealthy had reclaimed their property.

Chapter 20

In the year 2000, I had a difficult time coming to terms that the world was now in a new millennium and most ostensibly headed for the end of its existence. I felt pretty much alone. Since I had moved to Texas, my brothers, Darryl, Paul, and Robbie, were now 1,500 miles from me and weren't nearly on my mind as much when it came to looking to them for protection and solace as they did in the past. I now totally counted on myself, with God's help, of course! I never wanted anyone to partake of my agony, which seemingly I thought would lead to my demise. I was no stranger to danger as I ventured near and far in my apocalyptic trials—trials that I hoped Christ would soon deliver me from, in my mind and my reality.

It was a sure thing that no black hole, meteor storm, time warp, or strange porthole or any other thing, which unbelieving men could think of, would stop this inevitability. There would be nothing that would hinder the return of Jesus Christ, the Redeemer of men's souls, the Alpha and Omega, the Everlastingly Father, and the Prince of a Peace. He was undoubtedly returning as it had been forecasted by the holy prophets and apostles of old, for the signs were evident, not only on and in the Earth and the seas sustained by the remnants of believers, but also in the endless galaxies where inhabitants of other worlds proclaim and rejoice.

"Orion! Yes, Orion! Jesus will come through Orion!" I said emphatically.

Unbeknownst to the greater population of this world due to our own willful ignorance, Jesus's trek, through time and space, will begin in heaven. After he leaves the Holy of Holies, he mounts his interstellar spaceship with his bands of angels, with the mighty Angel Gabriel by his side and the two-thirds of the angels who remained loyal to him after the fall of Lucifer and his horde, the one-third of heaven's angels whom he had convinced to be on his side. Piercing through the sky that he created, after streaking through space with the greatest speed, Jesus, with all of his love, will and shall come in the clouds to redeem his own to himself with a great earthquake and with a great shout that all will hear at the same time all over the world, on the Earth as well as in the seas: "Awake, awake and arise, you, that sleep in the dust." And those trusting souls that believed and obeyed his commandments, who were dead, will rise and fly up to him in the clouds; and then those who believe, who are alive, will also fly up to him in the sky, all changed and given youthful and glorified bodies as he has.

"Are you ready, Darryl? This is what we've been talking about our whole lives! Remember in 1977, when you and I committed ourselves to fervently study the Bible, especially the book of Revelation?" I asked Darryl excitedly.

"I remember, Danny! You were eighteen, and I was sixteen. The zeal and fervor was sure in us, the Holy Spirit hadn't finished cultivating us," Darryl replied.

"Darryl, we've come a long way. God saw that we were on fire for him, and he helped us tremendously over the years, just to know about him and his wonderful plan. And now his glorious return is upon us!" I exclaimed.

However, I read that, the end is not yet. There must be a great falling away first, and then the end will come. This was according to the holy scriptures. Mankind will be so caught up with the cares of this world that we have no focus on God and what he cares about, and he and she will miss the boat a second time as in the days of Noah, for there will not be a third time. Those who once knew about God will lose their way of their own choosing, and those who never took the opportunity to give their lives to Christ will never find their way. "As in the days of Noah, so shall the coming of the Son of man be," states the Holy Bible. Before the flood, the antediluvian world mocked and scoffed at Noah's 120 years of preaching God's Word to them. And, therefore, they mocked God. They laughed Noah and his family to scorn. Even though they were forewarned, they made no attempt to prepare for the cataclysmic onslaught that would soon befall them.

Man will continue eating, drinking, marrying, and giving in marriage as if we've learned nothing from the days of Noah and that great flood, which came upon the Earth in the Ancient of Days. The same hustle and bustle we saw ten years ago and today will be an ever-increasing chaotic reality, and it will be even more evident at the brink of the true nonsecret rapture.

At this time, Darryl had become more prepared for the end of the world than me, his older brother, and also his younger brothers, Paul and Robbie. The window of opportunity was closing on us, and the Holy Spirit was steadily and diligently trying to get our attention to deviate us from focusing on the cares of this life but to concentrate solely on Jesus's mission and purpose.

Even though Darryl liked to dabble in the stock market, he was more aware of his spirituality than Paul, Robbie, or myself. It proved very well that the lines of communication were opened between Darryl and us. Darryl had to remind us of how strong we used to be for Christ's sake and how

Satan had beguiled us to seek gratification elsewhere. Yes, it was true! Darryl had to snap me and my younger brothers out of the satanic trance that the devil had put on us. Darryl was the most quiet of the lot but rebuked Satan the most. It was almost as if Darryl wanted to challenge Satan in mortal combat, as if he were the angel Gabriel himself.

Unbeknownst to Darryl, this job did not belong to him because humans (without Christ) are no match for angels, fallen or not! One year later, my wife, Fay, and I were extremely close while the turmoil of Earth's conditions worsened. Terrorist cells, corrupt politicians, and starving children around the world abounded. Ostensibly, I was rid of the worst nightmare I ever had. I was released from a hell that I never thought I would have escaped. I learned a new startling revelation.

My wife would try to save the world from utter destruction. Fay's scientific prowess had made an enlightening discovery. Fay had converted a spare room in our home into a planetary observatory and a counterinvasion shelter. She managed to construct a sophisticated tracking device that could detect interstellar activity as well as shield are dwelling. Fay had detected that aliens were soon to infiltrate Earth. She had given all who would listen an early warning sign, through the media, and a way to prepare themselves for the invasion. An incredible honing sound rang throughout the Earth created by the aliens, but the world ignored it. But only we (Fay's family) believed in her when the sonar device she created picked up on the eerie sound and traced it to its source in outer space. "Fay, you're a genius! But the government will not listen to you nor will our family and neighbors," I exclaimed.

"Danny, I can only protect us. If the world thinks I'm crazy and does not want to listen to me, shame on them," she exclaimed.

Days passed, then weeks. We never saw the aliens. We just knew that people kept disappearing after the strange sound that went throughout the Earth. At this time, there were fewer people in the world; however, there was no sense of urgency or mass hysteria, no panic, nothing, no news broadcast to inform the masses. Several months passed, and I left the confines of our home to venture out into the streets to see how people were doing and to help Fay get some answers to this phenomenon. As I walked around, I noticed that there were very few people walking about. The people I did see seemed like they were in a trance. I was totally oblivious to them. They wouldn't even speak or look at me. After several hours, I returned home and spoke with Fay. I told her what I had witnessed. Somehow the aliens were only interested in certain people because they soon stopped taking people from the Earth. And the sound that rang throughout the Earth ceased. Fay kept her scientific device on, just in case the aliens returned, but they did not return. At least there was no indication that they were ever going to return. The Earth never really got back to normal. After Fay, the boys, and myself had hibernated a few months, I ventured out again to see if the Earth had been transformed anymore. And indeed it had. As I ventured out farther beyond our street, I noticed that everyone I saw in our town had been brainwashed and in a trance. Everyone except on our street had a statue of a lady placed in front of their houses. The lady had a veil, whose garb was similar to that of the Mona Lisa. This was to pledge allegiance to the man who had taken over the entire world, the Antichrist.

The world was under his spell, and the majority of the people had the memorizing statue in front of their houses. Fay and I were one of the few people who did not acquire a statue nor wanted to.

During a journey into town, I discovered a mysterious dagger by the wayside in an area of town that had been laid to waste and desolate. I picked up the dagger and stared at its seemingly authentic qualities and surmised that an angel placed it there for me. I carried the dagger with me as I returned home. The dagger emanated a mysterious power that shattered the statues that were in front of the people's houses as I walked by them. I immediately went home to ask Fay and my son Demetrius to analyze it. They conducted many scientific and biblical studies on the dagger in Fay's lab and discovered that it was no ordinary dagger but that it had special powers that defeated evil. In her research, she found that the dagger was one of the ten lost daggers of ancient Israel during the times of the prophets Abraham, Isaac, and

Jacob. The daggers were created by lesser holy men of that time associated with the prophets to thwart off evil spirits that attack the camps of the followers of the patriarchs, but they were inevitably created for the future, for a day when evil would overwhelm the Earth. They were created to protect those who protested evil. For many months, Fay, myself, and the boys (Demetrius and Danny Jr.) conducted scientific and archeological studies at a time when the "man of sin" attempted to kill anyone who protested him and did not follow him or is his evil hordes. We did not fear this man or his hordes and continued our studies despite all we had heard about him. We continued to wait for the destroyer of the man of sin.

Chapter 21

I heard the voice of God who told me to prepare myself for his soon coming. I then visited my mother, Gina, before I had taken my journey to the desolate place he asked me to go. I told my mother what was on my mind.

"Danny, I'm so proud that God has selected you for a special mission and that you are going to see him before many other Christians. You will be in the company of great prophets like Enoch, Ezekiel, and Moses. Enoch and Ezekiel were our examples of the last-day Christians, who will be translated or caught up without seeing death, and Moses being the example of the righteous dead, having seen death, but being resurrected and then caught up first before those believers that are alive at the second coming of Jesus Christ. Either way, you come out a winner," said my mother.

"Mom, I can't imagine what God wants with me. I don't even consider myself to be a good Christian," I responded.

My mother packed a little bag for me, as mothers do, before my journey, and I kissed my mother good-bye. God had told me that when I was ready, to just start walking. I kept walking, passing all the houses and farms, and found myself in a remote and rural area, which had an open field where nothing was. And then, I vanished! A span of time had passed on Earth since my mysterious disappearance and news of an impending meteor that all the world's scientists concurred was broadcasted all over the world, on all television and radio channels and the web, that it was huge and quickly headed directly toward Earth in a matter of months and that we had very little time to respond. While the Earth's superpowers quickly got over their differences and formed an allegiance to fire all nuclear missiles at the colossal meteor, as a precaution, some headed to the catacombs and into the bowels of the Earth, especially most of the rich nonbelievers. Some headed dangerously close to the Earth's core. Mankind was going to be obliterated by the blast of the meteor if we stayed on Earth's surface or crushed underneath the Earth by the pressure of the Earth's inculcating walls of stone and rock from the impact of the earthquake-causing meteor is what every atheist believed. There was no doubt about that. These were the two major, secular trains of thought. And some that were totally confused believed both. Everyone except for Bible-believing, born-again Christians were utterly confused. It was a hard decision to make, or was it a meteor at all? The nonbelieving scientists were confused and kept changing their hypothesis. They had all of the nonbelievers in the world in disarray. Believers knew that when Jesus comes, he comes from the eastern skies and that there is a great earthquake first after he blows the mighty trumpet and shouts. Perhaps what the scientists and the military think is a humongous meteor is really Jesus and trillions of angels making their way toward the skies of Earth. And why wasn't it detected long before just a couple of months by the world's brightest scientific minds? Could it be that Christ was traveling through an undetectable black hole? So what is Orion?